# aLOha
## from
# HAWaii

By Bonnie Warren
Illustrated by Gayle Taketa

*ALOHA FROM HAWAII*

*Published by*
*WARREN ASSOCIATES, LTD.*
*4999 Kahala Ave., #453*
*Honolulu, Hawaii 96816*

*First Edition—1987*
*Reprinted in 1994*
*Copyright © 1987 Bonnie Warren*

*Printed in Hong Kong*

*With love to our son, Nicholas.*

We're off to Hawaii
my mom, dad and I.
It's my first time on a big plane—
I'm so excited to fly!

It's cozy on this plane
with these big comfy seats.
The stewardess said, "Soon, I'll
bring something to eat!"

My dad said "Look Nicky,
you can see Hawaii from here!"
I peered through the window
and saw we were near!

As we got off the plane
and walked down the stairs,
there were so many girls
with flowers in their hair.

My dad's checking in and getting our key. There's a bird in this lobby— he's talking to me!

*We looked at the ocean
from our great big lanai
and right up above us
was a rainbow in the sky!*

We built sandcastles.
We played in the sun.
We're really in Hawaii
this is so much fun!

The North Shore is where
we saw the big waves.
We watched all the surfers.
Boy, are they brave!

The International Market Place
has so much to see.
We took a pedicab there
right through Waikiki.

There were so many people of all different races. Everyone wore smiles on their faces!

Our boat moved so fast
when we put up the sail.
We saw dolphins, turtles, birds
and even a whale!

Penguins, elephants,
giraffes and monkeys too.
They were all waiting to see us
at the Honolulu Zoo!

So this is a luau—
a Hawaiian feast.
My dad did the hula—
and tripped over his feet!

Snorkeling at Hanauma Bay
was really a treat.
The fish were so tame
they would swim 'round your feet!

There is so much to do here in this land of paradise— Like eating teriyaki plate lunches with white sticky rice!

BENTO $2.00
SAIMIN $1.00
TERIYAKI $2.00
CURRY $2.00

Sea Life Park is where
you really must go—
Where dolphins, whales and penguins
put on a great show!

We pose for a picture.
My souvenirs in my sack.
I smile nice and big—
I know we'll be back!

I snuggle next to mom
in my big comfy seat,
and dream of Hawaii
as I drift off to sleep.